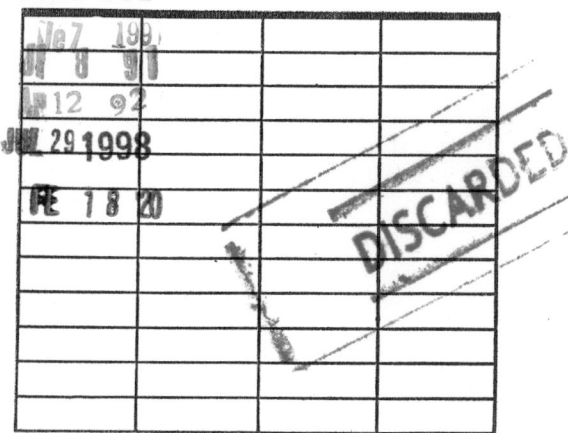

Notes for Parents

From a very early age, children enjoy learning the names of familiar objects around them. Talking about the things they use and play with helps them to develop language, which is such an important element in all learning.

Once children are able to recognize real objects, the next step is to recognize the same things in pictures. The *First Hundred Words* has been imaginatively and carefully designed to help young children take this vital step. All the pictures are clearly placed in a proper setting to make this task easier.

There are three main stages in a child's development; first, before children can talk they are able to recognize the names of things. You can say "Bring me your cup" and you will often receive the right response. Second, children gradually learn to say the names. It is surprising how many new words children learn every day. Third, children learn that real objects can be represented by pictures. Encourage learning by playing a simple game. Ask your child to name an object in the book and then find, or point to, the real thing. The association between the real object and a picture of the object is most important.

Always praise your child's efforts. It gives them a real sense of achievement to be able to identify more and more pictures. Little children love getting things right. The *First Hundred Words* , with such highly motivating, colorful pictures will encourage children to succeed.

This is a lovely book for babies, toddlers and young children to return to again and again. Learning the first hundred words will be a first milestone. Share it with them and enjoy it together.

Betty Root

THE FIRST HUNDRED WORDS

Heather Amery
Illustrated by Stephen Cartwright

Language Consultant: Betty Root
Reading and Language Information Centre
University of Reading, England

There is a little yellow duck to find in every picture.

In the living room

Daddy   **Mommy**   **boy**   **girl**

baby

dog

cat

Getting dressed

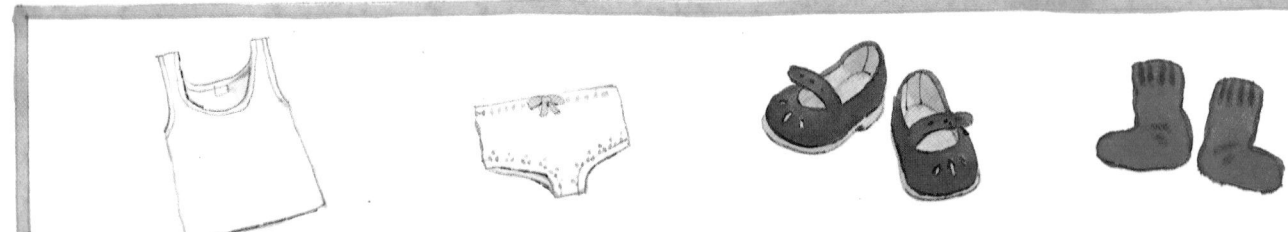

undershirt **underwear** **shoes** **socks**

pants **T-shirt** **sweater**

In the kitchen

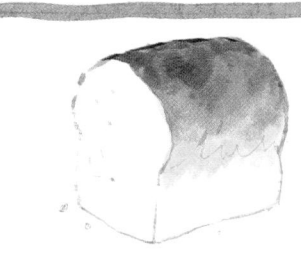

bread

milk

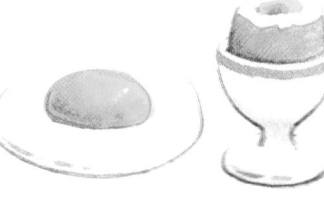
eggs

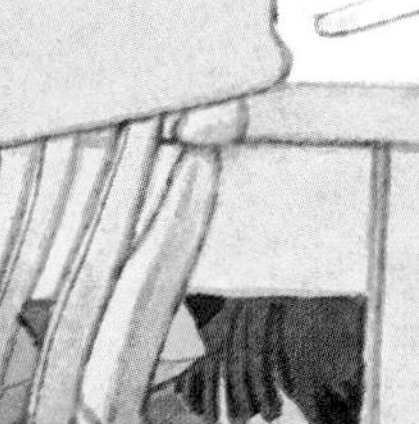

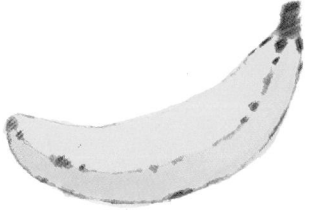

apple

orange

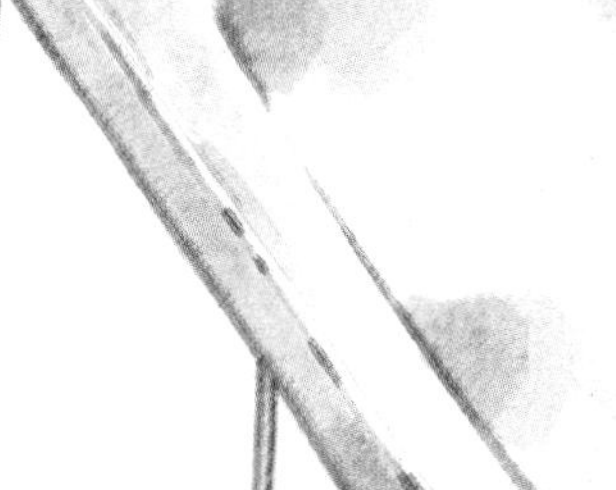

banana

Doing the dishes

table   chair   plate

knife **fork** **spoon** **cup**

Play time

horse

sheep

cow

hen

pig

train

blocks

Going on a visit

Grandma   **Grandpa**   **slippers**

dress

coat

hat

In the park

tree   flower   swings   ball

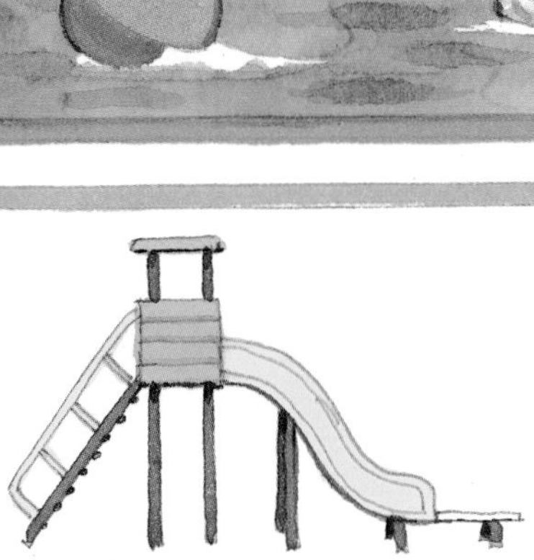

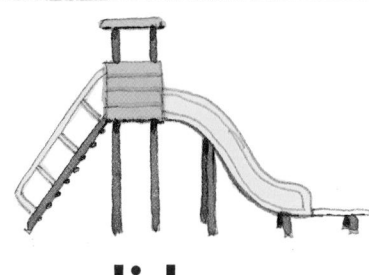

slide

bird

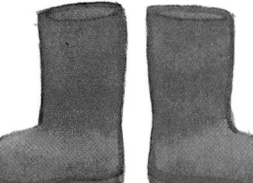

boots

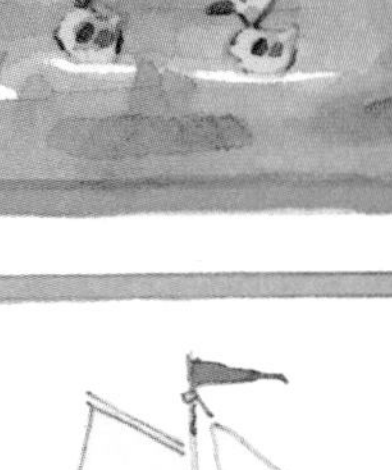

boat

In the street

car　　　　　　bicycle　　　　　　truck

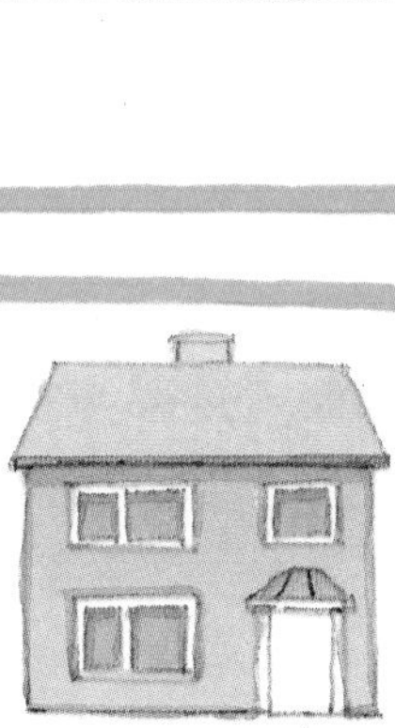

bus

airplane

house

17

Having a party

ice cream   cake   balloon

clock **fish** **cookies** **candy**

Going swimming

arm hand leg feet

toes

head

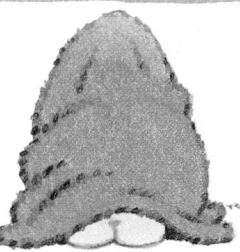

bottom

In the changing room

mouth   eyes   ears

nose   **hair**    **comb**    **brush**

Going shopping

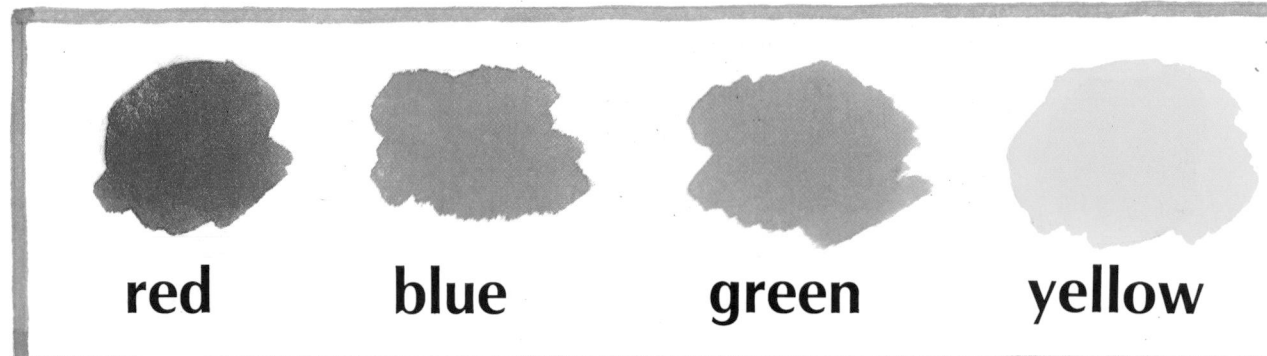

red blue green yellow

pink   **white**   **black**

Bath time

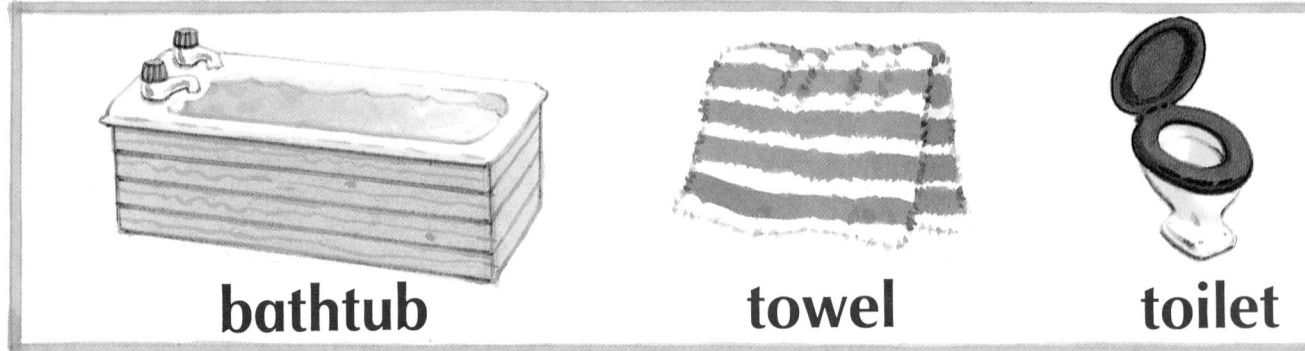

bathtub   **towel**   **toilet**

soap

tummy

duck

Bed time

bed **window** **door**

light **book** **doll** **teddy**

Match the words to the pictures

apple

ball

banana

book

boots

cake

car

cat

clock

cow

dog

doll

duck

egg

fish

fork

hat

ice cream

sweater

knife

light

milk

orange

pig

socks

table

teddy

train

undershirt

window

Counting

1 one

2 two

3 three

4 four

5 five

1 one   **2 two**   **3 three**   **4 four**   **5 five**